The Berenstain Bears®
and the
WISHING STAR

Stan & Jan Berenstain

Reader's Digest
YOUNG FAMILIES
Westport, Connecticut

One day the Bear Family went to the mall. As they walked past the toy store, Sister saw a big beautiful teddy bear in the window. It had brown fur, bright blue eyes, and a big pink bow.

"It's very nice," said Mama.

"Yes," said Papa. "That's a very fine teddy bear."

"It's okay, I guess," said Brother, "if you like teddy bears."

"Well, I do," said Sister, "and I LOVE that teddy bear."

"Hmm," thought Papa. "Sister's birthday is soon. That teddy bear would make a fine present."

Mama had exactly the same thought.

That night after dinner the cubs did their homework. Brother worked on a science project. Sister did flash cards with Papa. Sister was working hard on numbers. She had gotten a C on her last report card. Now she was trying to bring it up to a B, or maybe even an A.

Soon it was bedtime. As the cubs climbed into bed, Mama said, "Look! It's the wishing star."

"What's that?" asked Sister.

"It's the first star that comes out at night. It's called the wishing star because you can wish upon it."

Then Mama said the wishing
star rhyme:

"Star light, star bright,
First star I see tonight.
I wish I may, I wish I might,
Have the wish I wish tonight."

"Then what happens?" asked Sister.
"Well," said Mama. "If you wish
hard enough and don't tell anybody
your wish, it just might come true."

"I'm going to try it," said Sister.

"Go ahead," said Brother with a smile.

Sister said the rhyme:

"Star light, star bright,
First star I see tonight.
I wish I may, I wish I might,
Have the wish I wish tonight."

Then Sister fell asleep and dreamed of the big beautiful teddy bear with brown fur, bright blue eyes, and a big pink bow.

When Sister's birthday came, it was very, very happy.

"I got my wish! I got my wish!" Sister shouted when she saw the big beautiful teddy.

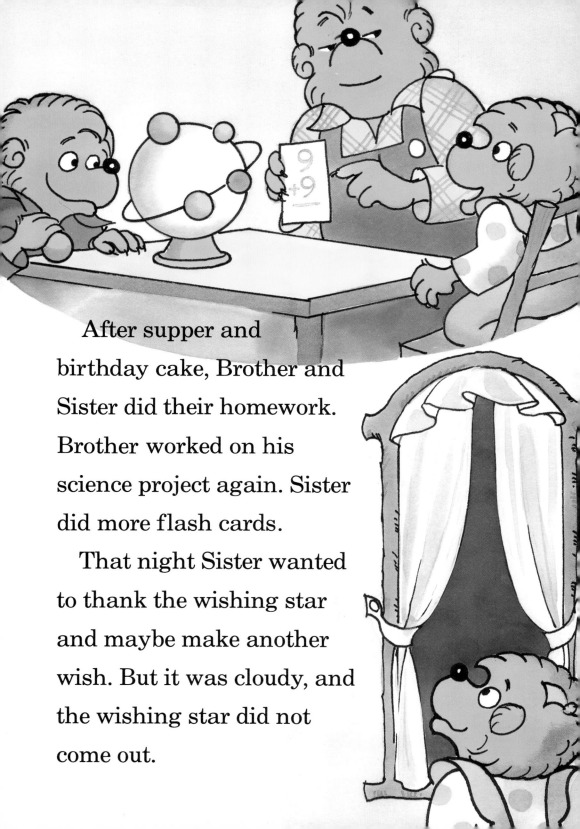

After supper and birthday cake, Brother and Sister did their homework. Brother worked on his science project again. Sister did more flash cards.

That night Sister wanted to thank the wishing star and maybe make another wish. But it was cloudy, and the wishing star did not come out.

It did not come out the
next night, either . . .

or the next . . .

or the next.

Sister began to get worried. Report cards would be coming out soon and she wanted to make another wish. She wanted to wish for a B on number work, or maybe even an A.

The night before report card
day, the sky cleared and the
wishing star came out.

Sister said the rhyme:

"Star light, star bright,
First star I see tonight.
I wish I may, I wish I might,
Have the wish I wish tonight."

Then she fell asleep and dreamed
about a B, or maybe even an A.

"I got my wish! I got my wish!"
Sister shouted when she saw the A
on her report card.

Brother had gotten a good report card, too. As a reward, the cubs were allowed to stay up a little later that night. They watched a special TV show.

The show was about a beautiful white pony with a long tail and a flowing mane. Sister fell in love with the pony.

When the wishing star came out that
night, Sister said the rhyme. She wished
as hard as she could for that pony.

Then she fell asleep and dreamed about the beautiful white pony with the long tail and the flowing mane.

When Sister woke up the next morning, she didn't even wait to get dressed.

She put on her robe and
rushed downstairs.

She ran outside to look for her new pony. She looked all over. It wasn't tied to the fence. It wasn't in the shed. It wasn't anywhere.

Sister looked very sad when she came back upstairs.

"What's the matter?" asked Brother.

"I didn't get my wish," said Sister.

"What did you wish for?" he asked.

"You're not supposed to tell," she said.

"You can tell if it doesn't come true," said Brother.

"I wished for a beautiful white pony," said Sister.

"Oh," said Brother.

"With a long tail and a flowing mane," she added.

Sister looked so sad that
Brother thought he should
say something.

"You have to be careful with the wishing star," he said. "You can't be greedy. If you wish for something that doesn't make sense—or something your parents can't afford. . . . Well, the wishing star just doesn't hear you."

"I got my first wish," said Sister.

"It *was* your birthday," said Brother.

"I got my second wish," said Sister.

"Yes," said Brother. "You worked hard for that A. You did a lot of extra work.

"But a beautiful white pony with a long tail and a flowing mane . . . I don't know about that, Sis."

"Well, anyway," said Sister with a big grin. "Two out of three isn't bad."